Rick Is Sick

David McPhail

Green Light Readers
Harcourt, Inc.
Orlando   Austin   New York   San Diego   London

This is Jack.
Jack wants to play.

Rick cannot play.
Rick is sick.

Jack can help.
Jack has a cup.

Now Rick is too hot!

Jack can help.
Jack has a bag.

Now Rick is too cold!

Jack can help.
Jack sits on Rick.

Now Jack is tired.
It's time for a nap!

A Friendship Award

Jack was a good friend to Rick.
Make an award for Jack.

WHAT YOU'LL NEED

paper

crayons or markers

scissors

glue

Draw a circle and ribbon.
Cut them out.

 Write something nice about
Jack on the circle.

Jack is
a nice
friend.

 Write why Jack is a good
friend on the ribbon.

Jack
helped
Rick.

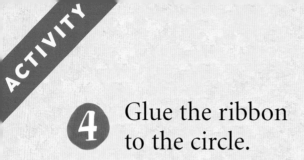

4 Glue the ribbon to the circle.

5 Share your award.
Tell why Jack is a good friend.

Now make awards for all of your friends

Think About It

1. What is wrong with Rick?

2. How does Jack try to help?

3. How do you know that Jack and Rick are friends?

4. What does Jack do when Rick is hot?

5. How would you help a sick friend?

Meet the Author-Illustrator

David McPhail had so much fun writing about Jack and Rick in another Green Light Reader called *Jack and Rick* that he decided to make them the stars of this story. He loves how Jack tries to help Rick when Rick isn't feeling well. He hopes that you help your friends when they need you, too!

David McPhail

For information about permission to reproduce selections
from this book, please write to Permissions,
Houghton Mifflin Harcourt Publishing Company, 215 Park
Avenue South, NY NY 10003.

www.hmhco.com

First Green Light Readers edition 2004
Green Light Readers is a trademark of Harcourt, Inc., registered in the
United States of America and/or other jurisdictions.

Library of Congress Cataloging-in-Publication Data
McPhail, David, 1940–
Rick is sick/David McPhail.
p.   cm.
"Green Light Readers."
Summary: Jack, the rabbit, tries to make his friend Rick, a sick bear, feel better.
[1. Bears—Fiction.   2. Rabbits—Fiction.   3. Sick—Fiction.
4. Friendship—Fiction.]   I. Title.   II. Green Light Reader.
PZ7.M4788184Ri   2004
[E]—dc22   2003012864
ISBN 978-0-15-205091-7
ISBN 978-0-15-205092-4 pb

SCP   17 16 15 14 13 12
4500561393

Ages 4–6
Grade: 1
Guided Reading Level: D
Reading Recovery Level: 6

Green Light Readers
For the reader who's ready to GO!

"A must-have for any family with a beginning reader."—*Boston Sunday Herald*

"You can't go wrong with adding several copies of these terrific books to your beginning-to-read collection."—*School Library Journal*

"A winner for the beginner."—*Booklist*

Five Tips to Help Your Child Become a Great Reader

1. Get involved. Reading aloud to and with your child is just as important as encouraging your child to read independently.

2. Be curious. Ask questions about what your child is reading.

3. Make reading fun. Allow your child to pick books on subjects that interest her or him.

4. Words are everywhere—not just in books. Practice reading signs, packages, and cereal boxes with your child.

5. Set a good example. Make sure your child sees YOU reading.

Why Green Light Readers Is the Best Series for Your New Reader

- Created exclusively for beginning readers by some of the biggest and brightest names in children's books

- Reinforces the reading skills your child is learning in school

- Encourages children to read—and finish—books by themselves

- Offers extra enrichment through fun, age-appropriate activities unique to each story

- Incorporates characteristics of the Reading Recovery program used by educators

- Developed with Harcourt School Publishers and credentialed educational consultants

31901059358202